Writing of a Stupid Insane Manic Loser

By

Braxten Hernandez

Prologue

A room full of stories that you have never heard because they were never wished to be heard. Not because it contains things that are bad, which they do, no because no one ever wanted to ask. A mind full of stories and a young man willing to share but no way of telling or forming the words that create stories. Dear reader, oh sorry it had to be you that heard these stories because no one else wanted to listen. Now that you chose to read a losers story now you will find a loser trapped within all these stories. There is a piece that you will find. Maybe it's insane or dumb i hope these writings will find you well.

Acknowledgement

I would like to thank myself for writing the stories and the person funding my work being my mother Roxanne Harris. May forever my name and my mother's be in a stories book

Dedication

Thank you mother for being great and amazing at the same time. You will forever be my hope in the face of crowds and other horrifying things that stand in between my dreams and what I fight for.

Table of Contents

Prologue i

Acknowledgement ii

Dedication... iii

Chapter 1: Introduction 1

Chapter 2: Now Through the Eyes of God.................. 4

Chapter 3: Peace in the Eye of the Storm 7

Chapter 4: Connected... 9

Chapter 5: Miracle.. 13

Chapter 1: Better to Rule Than to Follow?............... 17

Chapter 2: Unknown to This 23

Chapter 3: From the Insides.................................. 30

Chapter 4: Walk a Mile for Someone 37

Chapter 5: Ghost... 44

Chapter 1: Introduction 51

Chapter 2: Where Am I... 54

Chapter 3: Where Is My Daughter 57

Chapter 4: Oak Wood Police Department................ 60

Chapter 5: My Job 62

Chapter 1: Introduction 66

Chapter 2: The Problems...................................... 69

Chapter 3: Precious... 77

Chapter 4: New People 84

Chapter 1: Introduction

A long time ago, there were many beginnings to this decades-long war—strenuous and complex to many of the civilians who still wonder what caused the bloodshed of so many young men, men who now probably don't even have a mother to come home to. There were the Yankees, the Chinese, and the people from what was once known as Russia, now just another crater in this world that survived by little to none. I was a Yankee militia member of the Southern Union of what used to be Arkansas, Missouri, and Oklahoma. Most recently, we were fighting against the Federation of Americans for the panhandle of Oklahoma. They control Arizona, New Mexico, Nevada, Utah, and the biggest and strongest part of it all—Texas. They are one of the largest out of the seven other Yankee nations that once made up the United States of America.

I don't know much about the Russian or Chinese state militias or military men, since most of the Yankee states near the oceans have been wiped out. Fifteen nuclear bombs were dropped, destroying most of the West Coast and some of the East Coast of what was the United States of America. After the bombs dropped, the power of the nation slowly corroded, with many politicians fighting for fragments of power like two elk fighting for a doe. But slowly that faded away as people with military power started to step in. Disagreements turned into fights where guns became the deciding factor. Now I am just a cog in the machine, since all men ages eighteen to twenty-four must serve or be deemed traitors.

The war started before I was born, and now I'm forced to fight in a conflict that began with world superpowers that no longer exist. I wasn't high in rank because I lacked any thrill for fighting others over land that we all once owned. Thankfully, I was able to keep to myself most of the time, though sometimes I got picked on by the higher ranks. Those pigs died with the panhandle that we lost. Losing the panhandle was a great shame to almost everyone—except me. I didn't really care whether we defended it or not. I wasn't even from Oklahoma, so it didn't matter to me.

My name is Danny Veaga from a small town with its own military base called Altus. That's where my dad's side of the family resides. My mother is unknown. I like to think she was a dark-skinned beautiful woman. Dad never told me about her, but with my father being white and the rest of my family too, while I have a brown complexion, I'm sure my mother's to blame. I don't care that I was darker than most kids, but growing up in a mostly white community caused suspicious looks from all the old white folks. Then there were the Nazi fools who tried to insert themselves within the militia groups, though thankfully none of the Yankee nations recognize them as part of the political or military ranks.

What is left of this country now fights to one day reclaim all the states—by force or political means. Being a cog, I remain on the outskirts of the panhandle to ensure no invasion comes from the west. I write this to you now in case I die, since not just in the day is there gunfire, but also at night when nothing is supposed to speak. That is one thing that makes no sense to me, since in my family it was taught that when the sun goes down, you are supposed to be quiet so no man can hear another in case they are sleeping. With the muddy mold I call a bed that covers my position so no man may shoot me dead, I fear that an invasion is close—and I will die soon.

Chapter 2: Now Through the Eyes of God

The fire started slowly, encroaching on the position of the men of the Federation of Americans. The Southern Union made sure that whatever part of the panhandle they took would now be ashes. Many men tried to put out the fire—even men from the Southern Union—until they were told it was our doing. It still bothers me what we did to the people of the panhandle. Our own civilians died because of a fire so great, though we got some of the handle back.

It wasn't worth it. Just a couple miles retrieved back from those bastards. This was never worth it. I miss my family. I might just end up deserting and hopefully get back to them before I die out here in these dry hills. No one ever talks about how horrible the weather is here. The humid heat destroys the skin of many men on the battlefield. Others like me are called "darkies." I'll stop there before I get mad at what my skin gave me as a calling card.

I saw men burned alive through this tragedy. Animals too—shrieking for their lives. I never thought I would hear a mountain lion shriek, cry, and moan as it died. The sight of the charred bodies scared a couple of men weeks ago. I think that was three weeks ago. Now I'm stuck here waiting.

I remember what the couple said word for word: "The melting of the eyes was still happening. Slowly the eyes were there, slowly just… like candle wax dripping." The man who told us that was crying. What a coward, I thought then.

I've seen a fair amount of people die in my time. I'm twenty now, and I've been in this thing for two years. The bodies I've seen could build a house if stacked. At least one hundred twenty thousand men have died since the militia was born. Even though the deaths from my hand or those I witnessed aren't even close to making up that unholy number, I still had to see them. Blood dripping is strange to me. When you have blood on your skin, it's like it's trying to find its way back to the wound it came from—but when there's a lot, it just flows out like a dam that's been blocked for a while and suddenly opens. Blood flowing on the skin is the hardest part, too, because it not only stains the clothes but can also cause infection if you have a cut and it mixes with the blood of the men you kill.

Anyway, all the death on my hands causes me to weep sometimes. Yet it's nothing compared to what some of us have done to women. A couple of weeks ago, I raped a woman. I remember it vividly. Her hands were soft—her whole body was soft. I covered her mouth so she would stop screaming. I'm sorry for what I have done. It's just that I needed some relief. That's all it was, nothing more, nothing less.

I write this down because this will bear witness to my sin. The number of men without a conscience within the militia sickens me, but to think that I am one of them haunts my dreams. I'm not one of them. I can live with what I've done in this life, but when I die—hopefully soon—I can be judged by God and Him alone. I don't want the Son to see my wicked eyes any longer. It is said that the forgiveness of Jesus Christ is unstoppable against sin. If so, with the sin I bear, would He forgive me?

Chapter 3: Peace in the Eye of the Storm

On this day, we find peace for the first time in what feels like months—or maybe years. The Southern Union made a deal with the Federation of Americans: we would not fight if they got to keep the panhandle. I was afraid our ignorant leaders would deny the offer, but only a fool would do such a thing. Going up against one of the largest Yankee nations would have been suicide. Thankfully, that won't need to happen now. Hopefully, the peace will last until I'm out of this hellhole.

Now many people can stand up from the creases of land we call cover and not get shot. I tried it myself, and honestly, I felt relieved. I wonder if I had tried it before the peace if I still would have felt relief while facing death right in its face. No matter— hopefully we no longer have to care about whether we can stand up. Now we just guard the border in case something happens. Dreadful be the day if something actually does.

This week, the soup was actually good for some reason. Nothing changed with the recipe, but somehow it's better than ever. I get paid once a week, have my clothes cleaned, get to change my underwear, and finally eat something that isn't garbage. What does that finally mean for me, I wonder?

I'm an honest man who does what he can, unable to come to terms with who I am, but I feel a little free as of today. I always wondered what side of the tree is best to be on—the side where the sun shines or the side where the shadow falls. On one hand, the sunshine feels great in the morning and lets you play and run around. On the other hand, the shadow allows you to rest while all the noise fades away. I think for now I choose the sunshine. If the sunshine no longer exists for my future—so be it.

Chapter 4: Connected

Three months — it's been three months of tiresome freedom and I had nothing to write down. I wonder what peace is at this point, ever since the two militia groups allied with the Southern Union. It's great, but what does it mean for other Yankee states that are on the wrong side of this joint agreement between those war-hungry pigs? It's crazy how my two years of killing those stinky cunts — the stupid Federation of Americans. Stupid fucking names for countries. We used to be united, and now there are just ugly named idiots telling men to run around with guns for the hope of one day being united. It reminds me of this two-hundred-year-old movie where they make fun of religion, with men getting confused and mad at similar names of their terrorist group.

Now that we aren't fighting for the panhandle, I got some leave time and I spend more of my day with my family. I never remembered how gray the sky was; I never knew how clearly I could see. My father tells me the reason for the gray in the sky is the factories. Since the materials needed for everyday life are now either gone or replaced, Grandpa used to do something called "recycling" — basically reusing materials that have already been used. Why would anyone want to use trash for a replacement? It's a weird time that we live in, and since I'm a soldier I get to witness most of the weirdness first hand. Me and a private one time had to help some police officers arrest some men who were in love with each other. I don't know what to think about that. What did they mean, they were in love? I don't know — just something I often ponder. What is love?

I'm not the most emotional person when it comes to relationships or being willing to express my emotions, but I have feelings. I like to walk and listen to the joy that people experience and wonder what it's like to feel happiness. Why is it that others who haven't lost as much as I have are happy, while I wither from loneliness? Where do others come from to allow this thing that many men like me can't have? Saying that I have a conscience is ignorant and dumb. I know I used two words that mean the same thing, but that's how I feel — whether it's supposed to be said like that or not, I don't care.

Another thing is bothering me. This tall, pale white man walked past our house shirtless and barefoot, his pants made of a potato sack. For some reason, as he passed and I yelled out "Hello," he slowly crept his face toward mine. His eyes were red with a crooked smile covered in yellow. His grin is scarred into my mind, and that is something that keeps me up since I first saw it. I keep having this dream of a man chanting, "Beings that live without my knowledge live without my consent." I don't know what it means, but the dastardly albino roadrunner keeps running in my mind.

It's like a piano key that follows three repeated notes then ramps up into five repeated notes, all of them high. Seventeen men and women were lined up and shot in my most recent nightmare, with the albino roadrunner the last one standing. Death yells out in some of my other dreams, but for some reason my ears are covered while people stare at me. Darkness is a void. I wake up from my void and see a dark, tall-figured man creeping through my doorframe, then the dream is over and I'm in a cold sweat. I rejoice and fall back to sleep.

I think I have these dreams because I've also been paying for sex. A nice dark lady just turned twenty. I constantly wonder what would happen if my family finds out about my acts of darkness — that's what others would call it. But me? I would call them acts of desperation. People say that some things you don't need, but when you get to a certain age your body wants certain things no matter what.

I don't know what to do, but my body urges me to be masculine — either through sex, fights, or any other extra means of harassment on the female population. I don't know what to do with these thoughts, but at the same time I feel like I don't really care. Everyone else may judge, but they probably did something shameful in their past, so why would they shame me? Hypocrites are just all hypocrites. I would say that I fucking hate them, but at the same time that would make me a hypocrite too.

I think I'm just happy. What does that mean to me? I don't know, but my feelings don't matter. I have a couple more weeks until my leave is over and I could be done with this all — back to the old grind, as they say.

Chapter 5: Miracle

I survived being in a tornado. Literally flying around with my body flung at a speed unknown to a place unknown — surviving the winds. I was incredibly lucky because it sent me to a forest whose tall trees allowed my body to hit the branches, somehow cushioning the fall. My body is a mess though; only weeks of healing passed before my right arm was finally able to write so that I may communicate. My jaw was injured on the way down from hitting the branches.

However, one thing must be said: my family home has been destroyed and I am left alone in this world now, for what I know, since no one has come looking for me. Being stuck in this hospital has been horrid. The people here don't get treated right, especially the elderly. As for me, I've been treated okay. I'm stuck to a feeding tube, so all they have to worry about is the occasional checkup and changing from when I use the bathroom. It hasn't been mentioned yet, but my lower body is a disaster — I can't feel a thing down there.

I want to feel happiness. I don't remember what that's like, to be honest. I don't know if I can anymore. I don't know if it's a thing where I have to do something to make myself happy to actually feel it, but now, thinking that my family is dead, I don't know what to do. Even with my family, it feels like happiness died — my happiness, to be specific. I would put my hand in front of a burner to see if I could still feel pain, but every day I've been here is a reminder of that. A punishment, nonetheless.

Where is my mind? I wonder most of the day. I'm curious what I would do if I wasn't stuck here right now. Would I be my horrible self that I'm used to, or would I be the man that I always wanted to be, even though I would be stained from my past? Nothing changes the past, I've learned — or at least I think I have. At least I could pretend that I was a better man if I die.

Pretend — what does that even mean? Honestly, I didn't even think when writing the last line. I got so caught up in the affairs of my state or whatever this thing is that I protect, that I forget what other thing controls me to be this way. My emotions are the cause and the effect of everything I did. It's weird because there is this thing that the young generation does where they paint their nails black. I kinda want to do that right now, but I'm not a sissy.

There was this thing I did as a kid with my childhood friends — we used to smoke something that resembled grass and leaves and it would get us messed up. Such a calm that I haven't experienced in a long time. I wish that I could feel that again.

There is a story about people that once lived here before Americans. The story goes that a man had a system to hold him up. No way to take care of himself, nothing to fall back on — just a man in a world. Until the man met more men, and that man was provided for; with time, work and exchange of where he lived, his land became others', and he didn't mind because all of these things that were provided came to him, unlike before. The moral of the story is: until America showed up he had nothing, and that's how great we are. Where is all that greatness?

For the foreseeable future I don't want my memories anymore. I want to be a good man who can do things on his own. I will search for whatever family remains after I get out of this bed and make sure I can be free — more than I was when I was chained down to this thing we fight for. United for one is not united for all, and I'll fight until those words are spread across what used to be the United States of America and people know what that means. What does it mean to be an American in this day of age, when people are set against one another?

Two hairs pretending to be saints by braxten Hernandez

Chapter 1: Better to Rule Than to Follow?

Braxten died by his own hand. He wakes up with blurry vision but remains fighting the sleep by covering his eyes and wrestling himself. People walk past him on the cement not noticing or caring. Two 8-foot humanoid creatures walked over to him and started grabbing him by his shoulders, shaking him back and forth, screaming: "Wake up." "Hello." "Hello, wake up." "Welcome to Sincerity!"

Braxten was in between the both of them, half awake.

"Welcome to Sincerity!"

"What?"

"Welcome to Sincerity!"

"What's happening?"

The creature puts him down gently and waves its hand, and now the scenery is no longer a concrete district, but of grasslands far out.

"What's going on?" realizing that he was no longer within his reality. Mind over mind can't jump for itself.

"You were just in the concrete district, but now you are in the grasslands," one of them snarled.

"What is this?" Falling on his ass, backing up with his hands reaching back, looking at the creatures.

These creatures were at the very least 8 feet tall with turkey wings for a humanoid body. They were almost ugly somehow. If roses had a twin, it would question where it came from. Somehow it sang "find the words" while being able to speak. They laid out their hands so they could pull him up.

He didn't reach for the hand.

"What are you?"

"We are angels."

Confused and dazed when he heard that. It was a place so foreign and unknown to allow him to exist, he didn't understand it.

"What?"

"Angels, we are angels."

"Why are you always smiling?"

"Be honest."

"What?"

"Sorry, those are just those voices that appear from time to time."

The creatures bent down and looked at him.

"You are in Sincerity, a place where souls didn't quite make it to heaven but didn't do enough to go to hell."

"What?"

"You are in Sincerity, a place where souls didn't quite make it to heaven but didn't do enough to go to hell."

"Yeah, I heard you, just what do you mean I didn't make it to heaven? What do you mean there is a place besides heaven and hell or purgatory? Aren't those supposed to be where people end up?"

"Congratulations."

Puzzled with the successful loss, he was still in silence for quite some time.

"Hello."

"What?" he murmured.

With the eyes of an owl, the supposed angel stared at him. "We technically are no longer angels in terms of heaven, but we are angels in terms of humanity. We were fallen angels when we were kicked into hell but rebuked Satan after his folly, which cast us out as the ones who saved the men who didn't deserve hell but quite didn't make it to heaven."

The heads of the fallen angels rotated backwards to see a rat. Screeching, they ran after the rat on all fours, catching up to it and eating the unlucky bastard in one swoop. In an instant, they are back at the feet of Braxten as swiftly as sound.

"Sorry about that, sometimes the punishments from hell come and try to destroy the grasslands."

Breathing heavily, he didn't recognize what the fallen angels had said. Turning as fast as he could, he got up from his ass and tried sprinting away from them, but was stuck running in place, unable to make any distance away from the fallen angels.

"Don't be afraid."

A pause happens as they stare in the eyes of Braxten. "Wait, give it a second."

"Breathe."

He continues to try to run. The gusts of wind from their wings pushed him forward, causing him to fall flat on his face, breaking his nose.

"Listen, you fool," snarled one of the fallen angels.

"Be thankful," said the other one, slightly feeling contempt.

"I'm Augustus."

"And I'm Nepheline," said simultaneously.

Pointless since both fallen angels had every feature of each other.

Nepheline: "Look, you are in Sincerity, a place for people who didn't quite make it to heaven but didn't deserve hell." "Why am I here?" Braxten said while still running in place. "What am I doing here? I was a good Christian, wasn't I?" said Braxten, while slowing down into a jog.

"Nope! You did numerous things such as masturbate, be lazy, have anger spats, and etcetera, but who cares, 'cause you are here now."

"How did I die?" he said as he stood still looking at his hands. "Does that really matter now since you are here?" "I was a good Christian."

"No, you weren't. You barely read the Bible, never went to church, and sinned so much you would have gone to hell, but now you are here in Sincerity, and you're welcome."

Dropping to his knees, crying: "I was a good Christian!"

Augustus bends his body to be above Braxten and says: "Why are you crying? This is your heaven, where you don't have to be punished for what you did during your earthly mistakes. Mistakes are what they were, and if heaven couldn't see that, then better to live in Sincerity than to follow in heaven."

"I'm a good Christian," Braxten said as he closed his eyes with tears falling down, putting his hand in a ball, praying.

His pointless effort didn't mean anything since those who have fallen didn't get seen by the likes of the heavenly. He wept for five hours until Nepheline said:

"Are you done now?"

A sigh, releasing all of his sadness, came from him.

"What do you want?"

"Nothing, we want nothing from you, just to show you around the new habitat that you will be living in."

"Living? How can anyone live without God?"

"Let us show you how."

With baggy eyes, he stood up and put his hand forward into their reach, letting himself be taken by the two fallen angels.

Chapter 2: Unknown to This

The two fallen angels grabbed his sweaty and shaky hand. Looking right to left, he didn't know what was going to happen, but in an instant, they flew him high up, letting his body crash to the floor without a scratch on him. After pulling his head up from the ground in shock, he said:

"What? What just happened?"

"We took you and let you fall so you know there is no such thing as harm in this place," said Nepheline.

"WHY THE FUCK DIDN'T YOU JUST TELL ME THAT?"

"Be quiet and still, or I will make sure that you will be in hell," said Augustus.

Feeling nothing, Braxten shut up and didn't say anything for a couple seconds.

"Sorry."

Alone was the objector Braxten as he sat there with his legs in between one another, with his hands towards his sides.

"What do you have to show me next, and please do not scare me again."

"We have to show you nothing, but we will give you options on what realm you would want to inhabit since you will be here forever," said both.

"What do you mean, realm?"

"Well, this plane is only one of five that many others stay in. There are the grasslands, the concrete districts, the Heaven Walk, the Dark Descent, and Nowhere. Before we go to another, let's explore and find others within this realm."

"What do you mean by others?"

"Other people, you simpleton," Augustus rambled quickly.

"Is there any way to seek forgiveness within this realm, for I could go to heaven?"

"No."

"Well, maybe there is a way—"

"NO!" both yelled, as if a hawk was screeching.

Their feet bore claws, and Braxten was grabbed by the fallen angels, flying over some people within the grasslands. His arms flailed back and forth as he was being rushed to meet others.

Like a crane after catching its prey, the fallen angels hit the ground on two feet with Braxten laying at the feet of the people. "Oh my God. Why would you treat him like this?" said a man who bent down to help him out.

"Thank you," Braxten murmured.

He stood up and looked back at the perpetrators with a frown and turned back to the man, who then grabbed his hand and shook it excitedly.

"Nice to meet you," said the man.

The man was old with a great beard and was wrinkled and tall against Braxten's stature. He wore a nightgown that was the color of dirt.

"He must have been wearing it a long time," Braxten thought.

"Excuse me, but how old are you, sir?"

"Yes, yes my boy, it's been a long time since the people of the grasslands have had new guests. Let me ask the first question," the man said, then swiftly asked: "What is your name, age, date of birth, height, and reason for being here?" "Umm… Ok… My name is Braxten Hernandez, I was born twenty years ago on August 8th, two thousand and four. I'm approximately five foot nine, and I don't know why I'm here… I guess for being sinful."

"Sinful? You must be a Christian then? Come, I'll take you to your group."

He then proceeded to walk to another group of people, bringing Braxten and the fallen angel, and said to them:

"Here is your NEW Christian boy."

Then walked back to his group.

"Umm… Ok… My name is Braxten Hernandez, I was born twenty years ago on August 8th, two thousand and four,

approximately five foot nine, and I don't know why I'm here…
I guess for being sinful," he introduced himself to the new group.

The group welcomed him and introduced themselves while surrounding him and the fallen angels. The Christians chanted:

"MORE CHRISTIANS, MORE CHRISTIANS."

One of them yelled:

"HA, WE GOT ANOTHER ONE, YOU DUMB MUSLIMS."

Braxten then thought to meet the atheists instead of being a part of this group of people. He then noticed a third group, which he decided to sneakily walk away to, bringing the fallen angels with him.

As they walked, Braxten asked both of the angels a question: "Those weren't Christians, right?"

"What do you mean, they were," both of them said.

"How could they be like that? Christians aren't supposed to be like that. We are supposed to be accepting and welcoming to our neighbors? Those aren't supposed to be how Christians are, right?" Braxten complained.

"In life they followed God not because of faith but for community, and when God saw that, instead of how they loved others instead of Him, The Father, He knew these men and women didn't know faith."

"What is wrong with loving others?"

"Nothing, but when you are committed to something you shouldn't do it just because you have to—do it because you should."

"That kinda makes sense. Is that why Muslims are here?"

"Muslims are committed to faith, but ignorance is what brought them here. They are not here because they believed wrong but because they blasphemed against not accepting Jesus as the Son of the Lord. How could you revere someone but not know their title, Son of God?"

"I rebuked my sins, right?"

"A killer can rebuke his sins and be alright, so if you aren't a killer, what are you doing here?"

"I don't know… I don't remember how I died, but I knew I was a fighter… at least, I hope I was."

A quiet stills the conversation between the three as they arrived at the third group, with Braxten hoping that it was the atheists.

"Hello… Umm, I am Braxten Hernan—"

A sudden interruption pauses him, and the person says: "That is not needed here," and waves for him to walk forward.

Braxten couldn't tell, but it was a she; they were all women.

He scoffed:

"You aren't fanatics too, are you?"

"Why are you here? What do you seek, demon?"

"Umm… what?"

"You are a rat too then? Not sticking with your own, the Christians."

"No, no… it's just they umm… were not… tolerable, yes, tolerable."

"Then why do you think we are?"

Braxten stops and notices her blue eyes and says:

"You have really beautiful eyes."

"So the Christian boy comes here 'cause he is lustful then, I see."

Braxten, in shock, walks back a little, bumping into someone. "Sorry," he said, while quickly glancing back and then looking at the woman who gave him the accusation, now covering her eyes.

"Speak no more, for these eyes aren't for you," she said.

Grumbling with anger, she yelled:

"Why can't you men stop? First it was our husbands bringing us to this whole hell, then it was you men that always stared at us. We are not things of meat. We don't need you, so flee back to the dogs that follow, because we don't anymore."

"Shut up!" Braxten yelled. "All of this here, it's all new, and why can't one group or one person be normal? I'm a Christian, not a clown looking for attention, so please stop treating me like one."

He spoke, but she still rebuked him by yelling and screaming until Augustus said:

"Do you hear your call for war, Braxten?"

"All of you are cattle but don't have to be slaughtered, so why do you find an animal farm in a place where a sinner lies, to fight as if to fight off a devil," Nepheline remarked.

"Within you all, there is a tiny bit of evil that ate into your life, which caused you to end up here," snarled Augustus.

The woman exclaimed:

"YOU TWO HAVE NO AUTHORITY, JUST MAKING A PLAYGROUND FOR HUMAN SOULS THAT DESERVE MORE. HELL OVER HEAVEN, I REBUKE YOU BOTH."

Then in an instant, the woman vanished into the pits of hell, where rats will eat her forever into her ever-growing body.

"Don't be involved with things you don't have to know, Braxten," said both before he could process what happened.

The crowd in silence, the whole grasslands standing still, nothing dared move until Braxten nervously asked:

"Is there another group I could talk to now?"

"No, but now if you want, we can visit the concrete district."

"Okay… I don't think I'm ok," said Braxten as they left in an instant.

Chapter 3: From the Insides

Like a lightning flash, they arrive at the concrete district. Braxten arrives with his face flat to the floor while the fallen angels are standing.

"What the—why did I get a face full of cement?" said Braxten, while standing up and dusting himself off.

"This is where you arrived when you died," they both said.

A stroll between a human and fallen angels as they look up at the massive buildings that are as wide as a blue whale, with the smallest building as tall as the sky.

"Why does this place look like this?" Braxten wondered but also spoke out loud, with the fallen angels answering: "This place is supposed to be fit for modern humans, but don't be fooled, it is incredibly small. The max capacity of this place is 5 million, and somehow almost fitting that capacity. When you arrived, the people were out and about, but since it's nighttime everyone is sleeping within their homes," said Braxten while looking up, seeing the grey of concrete.

"Let's find an apartment and talk to the person within," Augustus scoffed.

"Maybe you can even get some shuteye," Nepheline remarked.

The nearest target for them to introduce themselves was the apartment building, where they entered just to see an endless hallway where you can witness the horizon line, and ceilings tall enough that Nepheline and Augustus could stand within. "What the—"

"The apartments seem endless, but they aren't, and most people are not willing to walk miles just to walk back and forth." "Back and forth? Where are they going?"

"Friends, family, others, etcetera. People really don't wanna be alone in their homes all day. Some say it is quite boring here, but they'd still rather be here than to burn in hell for all of their existence. Anyways, knock on that door next to you," said Augustus with a grin.

Knock knock knock

"Hello… is anyone there?"

They gave it a little bit of time until slowly the door opened, the crackling of the hinges being loud.

Yawn "Who can be at the door this earl—" shocked and eyes wide, the woman slammed the door loud enough to wake the other neighbors, with complaints coming from all around them. The fallen angels said:

"God, why doesn't anyone show us respect?"—then ripped the door open.

Walking in, the fallen angels looked at the woman backed up into a corner and they said:

"You, you are going to sit down and talk to this young man. Understand?"

The woman quickly gasped:

"Ok."

She sat down criss-cross, nervously waiting for Braxten to start a conversation.

"Ok… umm, what is your name?" Braxten asked.

The woman quickly said:

"Gloria Peck," looking back and forth between Braxten and the fallen angels.

She looked at Braxten, her voice shaking, asking:

"What about you?"

"Braxten… it is Braxten. Let me ask you another question. How did you die? Cause I don't know how or what caused me to die."

"Umm… I think I was murdered by my sister. It was a whole thing, but now I'm here."

"Wait—so you know how you died? Augustus, Nepheline, how does she know but I don't?"

The angels turned their heads like owls and answered:

"We don't know, honestly. It's not our call to tell souls how they died, and don't ask how you died, 'cause we don't want to hear it."

Puzzled, he asked:

"New? This is new?"

"Yes. Now stop asking us questions while she is right there."

Stiff as a board, arms to her side, she gulped and looked at Braxten.

"Umm… sorry about that. Anyways, why are you here, miss?" Braxten asked.

"MISS? I'm only twenty-two!" she said, while Braxten awkwardly backed up from her loud demeanor.

"Okay, I just had a woman yell at me in the grasslands, so please don't yell," Braxten said while looking at the fallen angels, then looked away as they looked back at him.

Braxten then said:

"Sorry, just trying to be polite. So anyway, why are you here?"

"Well, I don't know. The fallen angels next to you just blabbered out a bunch of sin, and I never really knew what I ultimately did," said the woman as Braxten stared into her eyes. "What?" she said to Braxten, who was startled, quickly saying: "Oh… umm, nothing… You really have beautiful eyes." "Thank you, when I was on Earth I was a model," she answered back.

"Oh really? Huh, murdered by your sister because she was just jealous then, right?" Braxten snarked.

"Umm… I don't know, maybe… Please don't use my death as a joke," she said back, now looking down at her arm with a frown.

Realizing what he had just done, he tried to comfort her by saying:

"Oh… umm… I'm sorry. I didn't mean to say it like that, just trying to put it into a way to quickly understand, ya know. Like, I didn't mean to hurt you. It's just that we are all dead, and I thought a little bit of humor would lighten the mood since… you know."

"Yeah, it's fine. I meet a couple of you jokers around here, and you're all the same. Why would you find death funny?" she said while still looking down.

Braxten placed his hands in front of himself and slowly turned them palms towards his face and just stared at them. "My mortality is still setting in. I don't know why I find my death or others' to be funny, but when I look at it from when I was alive, I found it to be a joke. When we die, we are no longer there—I now realize. Like, it's still a miss to me that I'm dead but still questioned about why I'm here. Honestly, this seems like a joke all into itself, that I'm going to wake up and go on with my joke of a life. Life is a joke, or at least that is how I knew it to be."

"Hello," the fallen angels said while looking at him. Their beaks slowly opened and murmured so silently it sounded like a mouse walking.

"Like a Christian that only believes in God for the purpose of getting into heaven, your folly is obvious," the fallen angels spoke up and said.

"What?" Braxten questioned.

"You heard us," said Augustus.

"The reason for living is for God, so by saying life is a joke is calling God a joke," Nepheline said.

"That isn't what I said. I said it felt like my life was a joke to what I knew," Braxten called out.

"You know about scripture and you have read it, and how God has a purpose for all of us, and you still called your life a joke," Augustus answered back.

"No, I didn't say it didn't have purpose, it's just—" Braxten was interrupted by Nepheline saying:

"Don't question God then."

Continuing to argue, Gloria looked at both of them and laughed, saying:

"Two fallen angels battling a human must have been a part of 'God's' plan then."

With the fallen angels turning their heads like owls, they just blinked at her—and she vanished in an instant, gone, never to be seen.

A pause happened for a moment, with Braxten shaking, knowing the fear that was taking over him but still resistant. He quietly said:

"Why did you do that?"

Looking at him, the fallen angels said:

"Love's gonna get you killed, but pride is going to be that death of you and me."

Glancing upwards, realizing what they just did wasn't just, and ashamed, they asked:

"Do you want to go to the Heaven's Walk?"

Putting out their hands towards him, Braxten, realizing there's nothing that he could do, grabbed and held on.

Chapter 4: Walk a Mile for Someone

Quietly arriving at the Heaven's Walk, the pair were being moved forward while surrounded by men and women walking in the opposite direction as if they were walking in place. Braxten didn't recognize what was going on, which caused him to be moved forward to the point that his body rushed another person, causing them both to fall, with the same happening again and again until Augustus and Nepheline helped out by picking Braxten up out of the stacked pile of bodies and pushed him against the ever-moving floor saying, "Walk." Confused, Braxten listened to the angels and walked forward while looking back at the pile asking, "Aren't you going to do anything about them?"

"No, they will eventually pick themselves up. It is their punishment after all," Augustus said.

"Punishment?" Braxten squealed, turning his head to the fallen angels.

"Yes. This is where those who felt that they did something wrong in life and wanted to receive some sort of punishment. So we decided to make them have to walk forever as a fair punishment. I didn't really want them to do this, but as the places got crowded, I decided that Heaven's Walk was needed. It was weird—sinners who wanted punishment, who would have thought," Nepheline and Augustus said.

"Why forever walking?"

"It just seemed right for sinners who wanted punishment. Let them chase the punishment they want versus what they deserve," the fallen angels spouted out.

Braxten noticed something while looking around the place that was infested with people who were all a few feet apart from each other. They were all wearing nightgowns.

"Are these people also religious?" Braxten asked the fallen angels.

"Yes, zealots that preyed on punishment."

"I guess that's the reason they ended up here."

"Well, aren't you quite the smart cookie."

"Thanks," Braxten replied.

Silence, with a vibration of the ground, caused the three to wonder what was going on. Time stood still for a second as a tentacle ripped through the floor, plunging many in from wherever it came from. The fallen angels didn't let whatever this thing was go rampant, striking it many times, many different ways. There wasn't anything for Braxten to do, so he had to participate within the Heaven's Walk, walking forward while the clear, blank, grey sky was filled with the fallen angels fighting off the beast. He sometimes would take glances back, looking at the fight between the monsters.

He thought, "What the fuck is going on? First I had this excuse for angels who would constantly snap and I assume kill people right in front of me, now there is a giant octopus thing emerging from the ground grabbing people. This has to be one fucked up nightmare."

After several hours Augustus and Nepheline banished the beast from once it came and arrived back to Braxten with an angered look.

"What was that?" asked Braxten.

"Sometimes hell spawn comes to destroy this place. Don't you remember the rat?" Augustus responded.

Then Nepheline continued, "Those that were engulfed by the creature now remain in Hell. Those sorry souls."

"This wouldn't have happened if it was more fortified," Augustus responded.

Nepheline quipped, "Oh please, with the sorrowful damage that you have done to that beast, then the damage would be lessened."

"What did you say?" Augustus angrily said.

Both of them clashed disfigured body to disfigured body, causing a strong gust of wind to push Braxten backwards, causing him to fall into the hole but thankfully grabbing the edge. While hanging, he heard yelling and loud bangs that sounded as if a building were falling. Hoping nothing bad would happen to him, he heard a whisper say, "What are you doing here?" Looking towards the whisper, he saw a giant eyeball with Braxten being not even the tenth nor hundredth nor thousandth the size of the pupil.

"What are you doing here?" the eye repeated. Shocked by the eye, he let go of his grip just to be saved by a hand that was pitch black as everything else in the area besides the grey sky from the hole that light leaked out of.

"What are you doing here?" it repeated again.

Falling to his knees, Braxten started to cry at the sight of the eye because of how big it was. "The endless building from the concrete district was shorter than what I can barely see of the pupil. Oh God, how tiny I am compared to the size of this beast," cried Braxten.

"Quit your crying and talk to me before I let you go to Hell," the eye said.

Sniffling and hyperventilating, Braxten cried, "What are you?"

"I am Nimrod and I am a giant," he responded.

"A giant?" Braxten cried.

"I said quit your crying now!" With a loud voice Nimrod spoke so strong it blew the tears and snot that built on Braxten's face.

Blank and still, Braxten, no longer on his knees, stood looking into the eye, shaking.

"What are you doing here, Nimrod? This is supposed to be this heavenly walk," Braxten bravely spoke.

The Giant laughed with water droplets so big launching towards Braxten he could drown in them. Once he stopped, he said, "Is that what those two told you? You are in Hell, boy. I'm the one holding what you call the Heaven's Walk."

"What are you saying? Sincerity is separate from Heaven and Hell," Braxten yelled.

"No, I made a deal with those two you humans called angels and we agreed that I hold this part of Hell up while separate from all of the monsters who once were angels, now beings that must be forgotten, for they could help me with my punishment," he blabbered out.

"What was your punishment?" Braxten asked.

"My punishment was to always continue to grow, every single part of me except for my bones, causing them to be crushed under a mass of skin, fat and muscles. What the angels are supposed to do is to allow my bones to heal to a fifth of what they are supposed to be compared to the size of my body." Being both deprived, Nimrod said, "I should have been the one crying instead of you. Unluckily for me, my tear ducts are sewn shut, for if they were to leak, it would be a tenth of Hell to be surrounded in water."

From above you could hear the battle stopping but still causing many people to fall.

"Giant, help me out. Get me to the Heaven's Walk so I could get back to the deceivers," Braxten shouted, pointing at the hole.

"Okay, but as long as you do one thing for me," grumbled Nimrod.

"What?" Braxten answered back at him, only for Nimrod to say, "Tell my story."

"Okay!" yelled Braxten.

Nimrod pushed his hand upwards, causing Braxten to fall flat until he was shot up 30 feet into the air when the giant blocked the hole with his palm. Nepheline quickly grabbed hold of him, gently placing him on the ground.

Braxten looked around for Augustus, seeing him sitting down with a pout. "I guess he was the one to lose?" Braxten asked, with Nepheline responding, "No, each time we fight no one wins. He is just like that because we couldn't come to an agreement. He always gets like this afterwards."

A chant around the fallen angels came from the people walking around them saying, "I will fall in the void just to avoid," repeated until the fallen angel stood up and took in a breath of air, slightly causing Braxten to fall back a little but being stopped by Nepheline's wing pushing him forward.

Augustus walked towards the two and nodded at Nepheline with a mutual understanding between them, being understood by Braxten looking back and forth wondering what might happen next.

"So I'm guessing that held on tight," Augustus said towards Braxten, with him responding, "Oh… umm yeah… no not really. There was a giant named Nimrod and he saved me and told me some… things."

"What things?"

Both the fallen angels looked at him with shock. Like when it sees its prey, their pupils shrank, targeting Braxten until he answered, "It's true that we are in Hell then?"

"What did that Giant tell you?" Augustus angrily spouted.

"A lot and I guess you already know what he—" being interrupted by Nepheline saying "Sorry."

He was gone from their sight, no longer being seen by either of the fallen angels. Braxten was now gone.

Chapter 5: Ghost

Pitch dark blackness—his body was no longer with him, just his soul covered with nothing that the eye could see.

"NEPHELINE… AUGUSTUS… WHERE AM I… HELLO?" Braxten shouted.

"What did I do?" he wondered while trying to look around, but nothing—blank nothing, something less than blackness. He would shout for hours and hours at a time, but once it felt like days he decided to stop.

"Am I stuck here? No, Nepheline and hopefully Augustus will come to take me back… hopefully. Do I continue to shout? No. It's been days and nothing—at least it feels like it's been days. What is this place? I can't see, touch, hear, listen or feel anything. All I can do is think, but I don't like the idea of being trapped within my mind. It reminds me of when I was alive. Maybe that is why I'm here. My thoughts were not just dark but horrid, causing my mind to have to fight constantly. Oh Lord, I am sorry for what I have thought, that being deprived of all humanity."

"You can't hurt those people now, Braxten," a voice from Braxten whispered out.

"Why are you here?" said Braxten.

"You have been so caught up in being dead that you forgot all about me," the voice said.

"You aren't real," he shouted to himself.

Continuing onward, the millennia of converse between Braxten and his dark thoughts could not be accounted for. The repeated cycle of beating the opponent, which was his dark thoughts, wouldn't be possible.

"I was doing fine without you until I saw you," he would continuously say, with the dark thoughts responding, "Say your stupid line again, beast."

A standstill between the two would not stop until Braxten gave up and, like in real life, the boy eventually faltered, letting the dark thoughts absorb him. For thousands of years he remained there, attempting to finally fight back but failing in his pointless endeavor. Pitch black void of nothingness surrounded him— even within the one thing that protected him, that being his thoughts.

A small dim light appeared and approached him. With his eyes dim, he didn't even notice nor care.

"Why is it that you are sinful?" came from the tiny light.

"What?" Braxten quietly murmured.

"Why is it that you are sinful?" repeated the light.

Finally being able to see, he opened his eyes and saw a tiny visage of a lamb.

"What are you doing here? You can't be here little lamb, this place isn't for you. I was sent here by two bedeviled angels and punished for what I knew about them. Go before they come for you and you suffer the same punishment as I," Braxten quickly said.

"Why is it that you are sinful?" repeated again by the lamb, with the lamb then saying, "In life you were strong to the very end, but at the same time sin would peek around you like a snake looking for its prey. Why would you do this to yourself?"

"What are you saying now? Why is it that you accuse me of being a little lamb?" Braxten said.

"Even now you let the sins of your past haunt you to the point that you were stuck in a cycle of guilt with you losing. You are like an alcoholic with how you constantly have to put away your feelings from the sadness that your mind creates."

"Why do you say this to me, little lamb?"

"Have you forgotten the thing that you have fought for, the thing that is constantly with you? You died by your own hand because you were weak and didn't understand every moment God was with you. Now you question me, The Lamb of God."

The moment that he heard this he tried to get to his knees, but now without his body, unable to move, his spirit grew at the realization that he was within the presence of God. Christ be the name of the one and only true savior that came after all the punished prophets that died for His name.

"Oh, be Lord, why be here with me, a sinner?" Braxten asked.

"Don't you remember any of my stories? It was told that mankind was to be saved, and they have been. Unluckily for you, there was quite some time where I came down for a second time, and finally Michael struck down the false savior, bedeviled into the pits of Hell, forever tortured for the crimes he committed unto God and humans equally. Since that has happened, I question why are you here while Heaven on Earth has begun because of what we have sacrificed?"

"Well, this is Hell isn't it?"

"No, this isn't Hell. This is Heaven which wasn't needed anymore after the promised land was created where God and I remain, no longer needing a place separate from humanity. Now the sons can finally play while the Father watches, enjoying His creation. But one son of God is gone now, with him that He misses and hopes the best for—and that is you, Braxten. Why do you do this to our Father, Braxten? Why do you hurt the Father?"

If Braxten was able to cry he would, but still he tried to, now understanding that he had failed the Holy Ghost, not allowing his spirit to be taken to the new Heaven where the Father missed him.

He cried out with no tears, "I'm sorry," and repeated it a thousand times.

The Lamb of God said, "Stop. 'Sorry'—I haven't heard that since everything has been renewed. I don't miss hearing 'I'm sorry,' but I do understand and know why you say this constantly. There is something that I must do before leaving now, for I am needed beside the Father where He is pleased. The former Heaven that is no longer needed must be kept well, and since no one else wants to keep track of this place, I want you to be a steward of this place where you will keep watch. Now that I say this to you, it is your burden to be here and mine and the Father's burden since one is without the other. We love you and always have and always will."

Finishing that sentence, the Lamb of God was gone, leaving Braxten bruised but warm with a blanket of love that covered his spirit, killing the dark thoughts.

Now alone in the darkness, the boy now becoming a man realized that the only way he could see was when it was bright, and so he reminisced on his good memories that he had by saying:

"Mother, I love you more than anything, and I hate to see you suffer. Father, I wish that I could see you more and love you like before the divorce. Brother, I want to go fishing. Joseph, you were always there. Colin, you were always so smart, I wish that I could know more about you. Essia, my very best friend. Manuel, my friend that I love so much. Austin, my friend I would fight for. Mohammed is the friend that I miss the most. Everyone that I love and everything that exists, oh how I miss you. Be it that I exist now in Heaven where I always missed while alive on Earth, now being deprived of the most true Father—even though I am now happy now, since there is no longer an end, now being forever where if I bleed I cannot feel it, only recognizing that I'm free. Thank you, Father, for I can love you more now and painless in the shadow of everything I am in love with myself, being no longer lustful. You have saved me."

Not the end, but now the forever love of Christ within Heaven which was needed.

Love,

Braxten

My Girl

Chapter 1: Introduction

I was always such a lonely bunch of characters stuck in one body. I always had a way of expressing myself, but I think this time I messed up big time. My name is Tex Wildway, and on April fifteenth, twenty twenty-five, I kidnapped a girl. She's around the same age as me, about twenty-one. What I did was wait until she went to the bar she frequents, drugged her, and then kidnapped her. Why did I do this? Well, it's because I love her.

Currently, I live with my parents in our old, messed-up house, where I've put her in the basement. My parents are old and they never go down there, and if they need anything, they have me go down instead. Me, myself, and I are the only ones who get to see her. That's how I like it, and hopefully it will stay that way.

You may be wondering—why her? Let me explain. I've known her for a long time. We weren't in contact recently, but we were friends once. In seventh grade, we were really good friends. I really liked her and wanted to be more, but she never liked me that way. That was fine with me, but to me, she is a goddess.

One time, we were joking with my friends and I saw a bottle of drain cleaner. I knew it was something people drink when they want to commit suicide, but I just wanted to make a joke. So what I did was grab the bottle—lid still on—and pretend like I was drinking it. Everyone knew it was a joke, but the only one to stop me was my friend. Oh, how I missed her for so many years.

To this day, that warm feeling—where she cares about me—keeps me up at night and gives me butterflies in my stomach.

After we stopped seeing each other—like when a friendship fades and nothing goes on between two people—I never stopped thinking about her. I thought about texting, calling, pulling up to her house, and so on. I really missed her, and that smile she had. Just the idea of it makes me happy. I don't care about all the others she's been with or how she's changed from the girl I used to know, but the fact that she's mine now makes me happy.

Her name is Jene Hill, and she's the most amazing girl in the world. I know "amazingist" isn't a word, but at the same time, I don't give a damn. For the first time in a long time, I'm with her. It really just sinks in now as I write this—she's with me and I couldn't be happier.

The desperation I felt while looking for her was harmful. Multiple times I hurt myself because of my actions. It took time to find the actual website to figure out everything about her, but thankfully, I found it. Three days of searching on the World Wide Web and I found her.

There was this feeling that once was a tingling sensation. It wouldn't constantly tingle—just every once in a while it would be there. It's still there, as it always would be. Tingling evolves, circulates, and goes around every part of my body. Many people unknowingly know about me. I am stuck in place, unable to breathe, just stuck with the people that have me with her. What was with her was a tightened bottle that wishes to be opened— and the bottle opens up.

Yeah, I guess I am a different type of loser. I was sent to do this. God has given me this purpose of finding my love and taking her for myself. The thought that I was given this makes me eternally grateful. The people who taught me about life would be proud eventually, when she is known to them. For now, I will let this be, where she lies unknown to them. I am in love with a girl, and God has given me her.

Oh God, what have I done? I kidnapped a girl. God… what am I supposed to do now? I can't do anything to her. I love her. Do I let her go? No—she'll tell the police. God, what have I done?

Chapter 2: Where Am I

Hello, my name is Jene Hill. I'm currently captive inside what seems to be a basement. I have no clue where I am. I just stay within this place where it's booby-trapped. My captor seems to be a masochist, I think? The stairs are laced with thumbtacks sticking upward, most of them old and rusty. My captor took my shoes so I can't even slam on the door for someone to hear me. There's a window, but there's an A/C unit screeching all the time, so I don't think people can hear my screams.

The only description of my captor I can give is that he's about five foot eleven, I think, and bulky. I can't ever see his face because he always wears this chimpanzee mask—like the one from the Bruno Mars music video. That's all I can describe about him. No tattoos, no scars, nothing—except maybe that he smells funny. I can't even describe his voice because he's always silent whenever he comes down here to replace the things I need to survive: a bucket, food, toilet paper, and a mattress. I used the mattress to stand higher to reach the window, but I'm still not tall enough.

I try to remember what the last thing I saw at the bar was. That's the place where I think I was kidnapped. It was a late night on a Tuesday when my friends ghosted me, so I was all alone at this old stinky bar. That just happened to be the day I got kidnapped.

This incident leaves me rattled, and every time I see that monkey man, it terrifies me. It's been about twenty days already.

The worst-case scenario is that I die here or live here with this creep for the rest of my life. I don't know how any person can take someone from their friends, family, and loved ones. Maybe a lack of friends that really matter is the reason this happened. Just one fateful day, and now I'm stuck in the basement of some loser who really has some problems. I also miss my dog.

I'm writing this now because he came down one day with a crayon and papers, which he decided to leave here in this hellhole. At first, I didn't know what to do with them, but then I thought about writing what's going on. Like a personal diary— but instead of writing about how amazing my life is, I'm stuck in a place where I'm being held captive like some freak in a basement.

One thing I forgot to mention: my father is ex-Special Forces. He will kill the guy holding me captive as soon as he finds this place, properly putting a bullet in his head for what he's done to me. Ever since Mom's death, he's been especially protective. This guy who's keeping me captive is screwed.

For my father, I don't think it was easy after years of service to come home and find my mother cheating on him. I never took her side. Even though she's probably thinking about me now and about how sorry she is for being the worst person ever, I still don't care about that woman. I just wish I could leave here as soon as possible.

It's not boring here, because it's not. He left books, games, and other stuff—which is thoughtful for a guy who kidnapped a girl for no apparent reason at all. One bright side is that I don't have to worry about the drama that was present in my life, which I really don't miss. Hopefully, once this is over, all this will stop and my life can go back to normal. Doing stuff like losing weight because I got a little chubby, or learning how to play the piano. Something poetic like that.

But if something ever happens to me because of this bastard, and you're able to find these notes, please be happy with your life, no matter how much grief you get from my passing. I don't know if I will die, but please—be okay without me.

Chapter 3: Where Is My Daughter

I'm losing my family. I cried out from my sleep just thinking about you. In my dream, she was screaming out to me: "Daddy, don't leave and promise that you would stay," she said to me within my dreams. I'm ashamed and forgetful about everything besides my daughter. I've been waiting, doing my own investigation for my own good, hoping I'll find you again. My daughter, I can't say how many times I've thought about you since you were kidnapped. It's been three months already, and your birthday is coming up. I don't want to celebrate it without you.

I remember the last day that you and I met. It was three days before the incident. I wish that instead of yelling at you about your mother being the way she is, I had shown you love—more than I ever had. My daughter, I didn't have to be crazy all the time with everything that's happened to me in this life, but now I'm stuck like this without you. I still remember the things we texted to each other the day before you were taken. "I love you, Dad." "Love you too, sweetie." That was all she sent to me that day, and now I don't know the horrors that have befallen her.

Now the worst thing is that I have to wait. Wait for many different things that could have happened to you. Oh God, I wish nothing bad has happened to you. If God forbid something—like even a scratch—is on you because of whatever you got into, I will find the person or thing that caused it and destroy anything that hurts you. I can't help these feelings that I'm stuck with, but what else am I supposed to feel besides anger and other emotions that come to my head when thinking of you getting hurt? Anger at the world for letting someone like you get hurt.

I offer myself, but even when you were little, when you'd get bruises or other things that hurt you, I would get angry that God didn't choose me instead, even if it was the worst pain any person could imagine.

As I record this voice message, I bite my tongue—a bad habit I have. Biting our tongue runs in our family, Jene. Your grandma did it all the time. She would just spout out words and bite her tongue often. I know you miss her too, but she's gone, and no one else was hurting as much as you were when she passed. I remember when custody was decided, and instead of living with me or your mother, you wanted to choose your grandma. I found it funny, but your mother didn't, so it made it better for me.

I miss you, baby girl. Just come back home to me, please. Honestly, I would see you later—if only I could see you later.

Now my heart is lonely without you and I can't think of what to do. I visited some of your old classmates, mostly girls but some guys from when you were in grade school, to see if they had seen you, but nothing. There was this boy named Tex who was really helpful and kind to me about my woes. I cried in front of him. I just started sobbing, and he cried with me, just there. Two supposed men crying like babies—but I guess that means we still have our innocence.

Jene, I honestly don't know if I'll ever see you again, but I hope I will. With everything, I will see you again, by God as my witness. You are going to be safe. I know you will. What else is there to say? But I know you will. I'm going to end this now. So please, be safe, Jene. Just be safe, Jene.

Chapter 4: Oak Wood Police Department

This is Sergeant Harris, and today I'm writing a report about what went down. On August sixteenth, two thousand and twenty-six, we closed shop on the Jene Hill case, now officially declaring her death.

We caught numerous calls from family members complaining about how the situation had been handled, but we aren't able to help with any further resources, as other cases have popped up involving missing children.

Being a father myself makes things difficult in this situation, especially when no clues have been found to further the investigation. I know if that were my daughter out there—alone or dead—I'd find the son of a bitch and put a few in his head. *Just joking. If anyone thinks I'm psycho, hopefully sooner or later, Jene Hill pops up—either in person or in a body bag.*

Furthermore, discussing the case without proper clearance to do so will lead to warnings and other disciplinary actions.

We don't know what happened to Jene Hill. We don't know if she's alive or dead. We don't know anything that could help lead the case forward—or even backward. There's only one hope of finding Jene Hill, and that's if she turns up—either alive or in pieces. Unfortunately, that's where we stand right now. Some people might call this case a waste of time because of the lack of evidence, but I want to emphasize how long we've spent working it.

No one looks forward to the days ahead, but we're out of time. We need as many resources as possible focused on other cases that are similar and still fresh, compared to what we've found with the Jene Hill case. From the day she went missing, she vanished off the face of the earth—and now, what sucks is that she'll likely stay that way.

I need to talk with the father of Jene Hill to discuss some of his actions that caused the case to go astray—things such as sneaking into homes, fighting with bartenders, and other incidents that harmed this investigation. I understand that he does what he wants, but sooner or later, there will be punishment for his actions.

No more *Mr. Nice Cop* trying to help a man grieve for his missing daughter. Now it's the *mean cop*—one who knows some of his actions have gone too far.

With all that being said, we're done here for today—unless anything else comes up regarding the case.

Chapter 5: My Job

Hello. This is my job—to document what happens at a crime scene.

On September twelfth, two thousand and thirty, a shootout erupted on a quiet evening, leaving five people dead: three seniors, one middle-aged man, and one middle-aged woman, both being around the same age. The gunfire lasted twenty minutes, and over one hundred twenty bullets were fired.

The names of the deceased are as follows: Tex Wildway, Mary Wildway, Joseph Wildway, Jene Hill, and finally, Tomas Hill.

The events unfolded like this:

First, Tomas Hill shows up at the Wildway household. He gets out of his pickup truck and pulls out an AR-15. Using the already loaded weapon, he points it at the house and sprays. Mary Wildway is the first one hit—shot in the lower stomach, piercing her kidneys. She immediately falls to the floor. Tex and Jene run up from the basement.

Joseph Wildway, being on the second floor, acts fast—reaching into a drawer and grabbing his pistol. Tomas then uses his second magazine and begins to reload. Joseph goes to the window, locates Tomas, and starts firing at him. Tomas ducks for cover while Tex and Jene help Mary Wildway.

Tomas reloads his third and final magazine, focuses, and shoots Joseph in the head. While that happens, Jene and Tex cause Mary to fall down the basement stairs after ducking from the gunfire—causing her to fall to her death.

Tomas starts tapping shots into the house. Tex runs upstairs to retrieve his father's pistol, only to find his remains. Jene grabs a knife from the kitchen and runs toward the front door. Opening the door, she's shot twice—but with adrenaline still rushing, she keeps running toward her father. Tomas stops shooting and lowers the gun. As Jene is about to stab Tomas, Tex accidentally shoots Jene in the head, killing her instantly.

Overcome with anger, Tomas raises his rifle toward Tex's position. Both aim and fire—Tex is shot in the head, while Tomas is struck by a fatal but not immediate blow. Tomas crawls to his daughter's body and lies next to her as he bleeds out. Cops arrive shortly after.

That being said, this was a complete disaster. Two accidental deaths. A link to a kidnapping that we believe to be the fault of Tex. Jene running at her father with a knife—while she was the victim of the kidnapping—may be explained by *Stockholm syndrome*, but it's too soon to tell.

And now, the news is all over this story. *"Kidnapper to Lover"* is splashed across the headlines, and I don't even know what to say.

All I can do is go home, relax, and hang out with my wife and
my girl.

Title: 12:58

Authour Braxten Hernandez

Chapter 1: Introduction

At 12:58, a boy wakes up in the middle of the night with a cold sweat, breathing heavily. Shirtless and pantless, wearing only his underwear, he gets up out of his bed and walks towards his window to look out. Nothing is there, just his backyard covered in dog toys and other stuff you would find in the backyard of a dog lover. Both of the dogs that were on his bed stand up and sniff him, wondering if he was alright. Turning back towards the bed, the boy pets both of them softly and proceeds to walk to his hallway.

He enters his hallway, letting the dogs follow him while walking to his kitchen. The dogs start to jump around, excited to be in the living room. Toys are scattered throughout the living room, only stopping once the interconnected living room and kitchen reach the refrigerator. Within the refrigerator are multiple types of meat, multiple types of vegetables, and multiple types of liquids. Nothing processed, just pure food, as some would call it.

The boy opens the refrigerator and grabs water from the bottom shelf and quickly chugs the whole bottle right there. He walks towards his trash can but slips on a dog toy, causing him to crack his head open. He wakes up after 12 hours of rest on the kitchen floor. Both of the dogs, sleeping right next to him, slowly get up. His head hurts. The boy then walks towards his room to retrieve his phone to call an ambulance. Blood drips from his head while walking, causing the dogs to sniff or lick some of the blood that ends up on the floor.

The ambulance arrives, and they find the boy resting on his front porch with his head being held up by his arm so he wouldn't fall unconscious. Immediately, the boy is rushed inside the ambulance and treated as anyone with a head injury would. Rushing towards the hospital, the ambulance was hit by another ambulance. Both of the ambulances, going over 50 miles per hour, caused quite the stir within the intersection. Both of the drivers of the ambulances are dead, with the passengers of the incident remaining injured. Cops coming up to the scene see the massive gore that the front of the collision caused. One of them threw up at the sight of a mangled head that looked as if it exploded. The boy, confused as to who he is, walks out of the ambulance and sits on the curb and is questioned by the police while making sure that the boy was alright. After another ambulance arrived, it goes and takes the boy for treatment at the nearby hospital, then the psych ward after the boy cannot recall his memory.

The last thing that he remembered after the incident was that he had dogs, and multiple dogs were brought in to help the boy with his memory so he could recollect who he was. Nothing was working until he saw one of the poodles that was brought in and it sniffed his hand. Emotions and memories rush through him, and he was quickly discharged and released from the hospital.

Rushing home, he was happy but worried for his dogs. With justified worries, he was happy once he came home to both of his dogs, emaciated but alive, getting excited when they saw him. Then they were quickly fed and were alright.

Chapter 2: The Problems

One thing that the boy didn't realize because he was worried about his dogs was the fact that the door was left unlocked, with the whole world willing to enter. Noise erupts within the bedroom. It scares the boy, and slowly he walks towards the place that it came from, that being the bedroom. Slowly walking there gives him anxiety, the dogs barking, causing him to yell at them, "Shut up." The boy slowly opens the door to his bedroom, where he finds a man sprawled out on his bed with his head blown off.

On the walls are words written with blood saying, "Hell has come for me, and now in this empty house, it is now mine." At the sight that he sees the gore, he screams, running away. He quickly closes the door and calls the police. He waits 10 minutes on the curb in front of the house, where he is arrested but let go since he had an alibi from being at the hospital. He was quickly told to get the dogs and some of the belongings like his toothbrush, charger, and stuff like that.

Two weeks later after the incident, the boy arrives home with his dogs to a fresh and clean house. His bedroom, he thought, thankfully was cleaned and had a new bed with bedsheets. The dog's excitement immediately ruins the bed. There was no smell of dogs either. It was strange for the first time in a long time to have a household that didn't feel like a dog house, but he was also distracted by the fact that he had to buy new groceries.

Night came and he kind of didn't want to sleep. The thought of a dead man within his room scared him. He slowly lays down and tells his dogs to get on the bed. Both of them jump onto the bed, scooching their butts towards the end of the bed. Being scared, he turns on his TV and lets it play as he tries to go to sleep. Closing his eyes, he can hear his dogs snoring while he tries to sleep.

Suddenly, thunder. The boy and the dogs erupt from the bed, screaming and barking, scared out of their minds. The boy turns on the lights and looks around his room to make sure that no one is within his home. Scared, he decided to go within the house and make sure that everything was locked. Room to room, he turns the lights on for each dark room, making sure that doors and windows are locked. With every creak, the boy jumps, causing him to back up but push forward to eventually clear the room. Sooner rather than later, all the rooms inside the house were checked, with them being safe.

After checking the rooms, he sits down on his couch, tired, turns on the TV, and just watches funny YouTube videos. As it started pouring outside, during the time where he dozed off, a single piece of paper was blown down in front of him from the countertop. On that piece of paper, a doodle from the boy was drawn. The piece of paper stays there until eventually the boy wakes up, standing up, and nearly slipping on the paper. The boy thought to himself, "Fuck, nearly another accident. I need to be more careful."

The boy picks up the piece of paper and puts it in the trash. The trash was clean, as if the people who cleaned the house even did the boy a favor by taking out the trash. He was thankful and decided to go and get groceries, so he got dressed for the store. He puts on a blue tank top and shorts, and because of the fact he lived in Arizona during a summer, he was pretty sure that he would be alright. As soon as he left his front door and locked it, the boy felt a chill pass by him.

Grabbing numerous things to fill his refrigerator, he spends $300 just on meat. Once he arrived back at his car, for some reason the car windows were foggy, and even though he rubbed the window, it refused to even smudge. Only when he opens the door does a weird breeze push forward. He thought it was weird but didn't really care. Often stupidity is involved with ignorance, but in this case, stupidity is just stupidity.

Leaving the parking lot, the boy then faces an intersection, and when the light turns green, he drives as he should, but as soon as he leaves the middle, a car running the light gets hit by a car behind him. He looks back but makes sure that another accident doesn't happen by keeping his eyes on the road. "Jeez, what was that about? Maybe just another stupid driver," he thought while looking at his mirror, slightly drifting to the left, causing him to swerve back into his lane. Then he arrives back at home, pondering what happened within the day.

As soon as he steps outside his car, he slips and falls on his face, causing his nose to bleed. He forgets the groceries and goes inside the house and grabs his tissues. Quickly he plugs up his nose while pinching, stopping the bleeding as soon as five minutes passed. He realizes that he left the groceries, so he grabs them and puts them away. He calls for his dogs, but only one arrives. He looks for the other one and finds her whimpering in a corner. "What's wrong, buddy?" he says to the now bowing dog. The boy then tries to move the dog, but she won't budge. So the boy grabs the treat that was for the dog and leaves it a couple feet from where she would stay.

Night came and the dog was still there. The boy worried, so he decided to sleep in the living room with the dog. He got ready for the night by bringing his blanket and pillow to the living room. He stripped to his underwear and laid down on the couch, covered by his blanket in comfort, watching television. Quickly he falls asleep with the television playing. Static erupts from the television, scaring the dog, but the boy, still asleep, moves a little but is really unfazed.

The dog snarls while the TV continues to make static noise, now changing channels since the boy is sitting on the remote, causing words to be jumbled up from words off of television shows, saying, "My... numb... hand... is... falling... off... Oh...

God… what… have… I… done." Immediately, the static is gone, the changing of channels is done, and the television turns off with the dog going underneath the blanket, hiding from whatever thing it was scared of.

Hours pass, and it's morning again. Waking up hot, covered by fur, the boy wonders, "What are you underneath the blankets?" Swiftly he removes his blankets, goes to his room, gets dressed, and gets ready for work. Shaving, brushing his teeth, and not forgetting to show of course. He works in a cubical, writing off people's insurance claims so the company could save money. He didn't like his job, but the money was too good for him to give it up. Walking towards his car after locking the door to his house, he notices that the windows are clear this time. He thinks, "Thankfully, nothing is wrong with my car. I just forgot to turn off the car and left the car really cold."

The house, now empty of human life, just with dogs, is cheerful. One dog tries to get the other dog to move from her spot, but she wouldn't budge. Bringing toys to see if they want to play tug of war, but still the dog doesn't move, just stays still and starts to whimper. The other dog turns his head to wonder what is wrong. The television turns on in the other room. One of the dogs starts to bark, and the other is not caring. The dog in the corner turns and faces the wall, and when the other dog approaches him, she gets bit from the dog in the corner, causing the other dog to bleed. Afterwards, the other dog goes to the living room and licks his wound, accidentally sitting on the remote.

The TV turns off and on a news segment talking about the up-and-coming elections. The TV blaring with an interval saying, "My... people... my... son... fight... free... other... live... sure... please... fight." Suddenly the toaster goes off without anyone starting it. Things fall from the countertop. The scared dog tries to hide its head underneath the carelessly left blankets. Noise all around the room. The dog that was in the corner now arrives in the living room, snarling and looking at the dog that is hiding. The snarling dog jumps on the one in the blankets, starting a fight. Both fighting tooth and nail, the scared dog is barely able to fight off the snarling dog but still holds off. The front door unlocks, then opens, where the snarling dog, covered in blood, runs off into the neighborhood.

People playing outside are attacked. Kids and women are bitten, mostly with minor bites, until one child was bitten on the neck with the dog holding on even as the parents attack him to get off of their son. Five minutes pass, and the boy, unable to breathe, dies from suffocation. As soon as he is done with the boy, he attacks the parents, but only doing minor damage. It is only until one of the old neighbors brings out a 12-gauge shotgun and shoots the dog as the dog approaches to attack. The dog, with its body in shambles, dies with its tongue out, covered in blood.

Police arrive too little, too late. They go over what happened and find the boy's house empty without him. Only the dog, bleeding and liking its wounds, crying from the battle that she had from the evil and monstrous dog, is now the only of the two left. They get a hold of the boy's phone number, and he rushes home. On the way, he passes by the house where his dog was shot, and he starts to cry. Pushing further, he arrives at his house and finds that some police have taken his other dog to the vet while others wait for him to arrive at his home.

"WHAT'S GOING ON?" the boy says. "Sir, we need to ask you some questions." "WHERE IS MY DOG?" "Your dog's alright, just a few wounds, but it doesn't matter right now. A child's dead and others are injured, so we want to know about the dog that caused the incident. Did he have an infectious disease that many of the people who bit have to worry about?" "WHAT ARE YOU TALKING ABOUT?" "Please calm down. We are going to take you in for questioning at the police station. So either come with us, or we are going to put you in handcuffs." "WHAT, NO!" "Okay, Jerry, put him in cuffs. We are charging you for manslaughter for what happened today. You fucked up leaving your door open, bub."

Then he was arrested where a little scuffle broke out, leading to the boy getting a broken nose and charged with resisting arrest. Arriving at the police station with hours and hours of questioning, he finally gets his one phone call to the vet regarding his dog, telling them to keep her overnight to make sure she was all good. Wasting his only phone call on a dog was a stupid action, but to him, he loved that dog, so the fact that she could end up dead scared him. Going back to the holding cell, he was let go after a camera from a neighboring house in front of his showed footage of him locking and closing the door, making the possibility of manslaughter implausible.

First, he picked up his now only dog from the vet and made sure she was alright. She was covered in bandages, but still, she was excited to see him. Unable to move how she used to, she started licking the air when she saw him instead of jumping on him. The boy walks slowly and gently pets his dog, crying, thinking about the other dog that is now dead. He asks the vet if everything is alright with her but stutters a little towards the end of the sentence. The vet responds, "Yes, she is alright. She just has to take some antibiotics and other pills to make sure that she either doesn't get an infection or stuff like that." Thankful, he takes his dog home, not ready for the hell to come.

Chapter 3: Precious

When they both arrived home, the dog didn't want to go inside the place it once considered its home. The boy went in, grabbed a treat, and persuaded the dog to come in. The dog approached the living room and whimpered. The boy comforted her and cried alongside her, falling to his knees and sobbing for a while—until he heard a noise coming from his bedroom.

A scream erupted from the kitchen. Quickly, the boy ran to check it out—but there was nothing. Confused, he calmed himself and walked back to his now frightened dog.

Gently brushing her snout, he said, "It's alright, just a loud noise." The dog whimpered softly, then stopped as he guided her to the couch. They both sat down in front of the television and began watching their programs.

While sitting there, the boy received a call from work. They had been bombarding his phone, worried about why he had gone home so early. Calmly, he explained the situation and requested a few days off to care for his only dog. After hearing what he'd been through, and following some discussions with management, they allowed him three days off.

Now able to relax, he watched *SpongeBob* while petting his dog. Yes—a grown man watching a children's show. Hours passed with nothing but the TV blaring and him scrolling on his phone. Eventually, he decided to go to sleep. Instead of sleeping in silence, he left some music playing. To him, it was smooth music—but most would consider it depressing.

He stripped down to his underwear, got into bed, and lay next to his dog. Blinking slowly, he drifted toward sleep—what many might consider the closest thing to death.

The perspective shifts—starting beside his head, moving to the foot of the bed, then slowly panning upward as if filmed by a shaking camera. The boy and the dog come into view. The dog opens her eyes and starts to snarl while the boy sleeps. She doesn't move but stands her ground. The "camera" pans over the boy as the dog suddenly runs to the bedroom door, scratching desperately to escape. She fumbles with the handle and, luckily, manages to open it.

Suddenly, the boy wakes with a silent scream. He jerks around, clutching his neck—he can't breathe. Panicking, he thrashes side to side, gasping for air. He sits up and flails on the bed. From the next room, the sound of the shower turning on echoes faintly. For twenty long seconds, he struggles for breath. Desperate, he bashes his body against the wall, finally managing to draw in a small gulp of air. Realizing this, he slams himself into the wall again and again—six times—leaving a dent the size of his upper body. On the seventh impact, he begins to breathe again, though he's hyperventilating from lack of oxygen.

Leaning back against the wall, he slowly regains control of his breathing before passing out, somewhat stable. The dog stops scratching at the door and turns, looking at her owner. She slowly walks over and lies down on his lap, falling asleep.

The shower continues to run, steam filling the air. Suddenly, a loud, discordant noise erupts—like a band of trumpets blowing at once. Whimpering, the dog doesn't know what to do. She stays beside her owner, closing her eyes, waiting for it to end.

Abruptly, the noise stops. Silence. Then, the TV turns on.

Just like before, the channels flick rapidly, forming a message: **"We... Are... One... We... Are... Many... We... Are... Legion."**

The TV switches off. The shower stops.

Moments later, the boy and the dog begin to float. The dog barks frantically, unable to control her movements. Both of them hover for a moment before dropping back onto the bed. The dog stands on her owner's chest, barking toward the ceiling— for hours.

Annoyed, a neighbor comes over to complain about the noise.

He knocks. No answer. Knocks again. Still nothing. The dog stops barking. Satisfied, the neighbor turns to leave. As he reaches the sidewalk, the house door creaks open. He looks back and sees only darkness in the doorway.

A hollow voice calls out: "Come in."

"Look, bub," the neighbor snaps, "I just wanted to tell you to shut your fucking dog up. I'm not coming inside your house."

Silence for fifteen seconds.

"Fuck this," the neighbor mutters and turns to leave—when suddenly he's yanked backward, falling hard on his backside. He's dragged slowly toward the house.

"HELP! HELP! MY FUCKING NEIGHBOR IS CRAZY!" he screams, but the pulling quickens, scraping his back across the ground. He's dragged up the single step into the house, skin tearing and splinters embedding in his back. His shirt rides up as he's pulled across the hardwood and finally into the carpeted living room, where the dragging stops.

He scrambles to his feet, limping, and rushes to the front door. It won't open. He pounds on it over and over. No use.

Then, that same hollow voice whispers, "Come here."

Panicking, he backs up against the wall and winces as pain shoots through the raw skin on his back. Breathing heavily, he steadies himself and peers toward the living room. His fingernails are too damaged to rub his eyes, so he blinks rapidly, trying to focus. Step by step, he moves forward on the balls of his feet, his heels too blistered to bear weight.

He hears the whisper again—this time multiplied—"Knife…"

The interconnected living room and kitchen erupt in chaos. Things crash to the floor; cabinets slam open and shut. Lights flicker violently.

"WHAT THE FUCK IS GOING ON?" he shouts.

Everything stops—except the cabinet where the knives are stored. It continues to rattle. He walks toward it and closes it, stopping the noise.

Then, again, a whisper: "Knife."

He spins around, terrified, scanning the room. Thinking fast, he grabs a knife, clutching it tightly in both hands. Carefully, he searches the house, trying to pry open windows or doors, but nothing gives way.

When he reaches the master bedroom, the door is wide open. The light is on, but the bed is hidden by a wall near the entrance. As he steps inside, he sees them—the boy and the dog—unconscious.

"What is going on?!" he yells.

The TV flickers on again, showing *The Exorcist*. It's at the scene where the priests attempt to cast out the demon. Their shouts are distorted, the volume rising until the sound becomes unbearable. He covers his ears, but it doesn't help. The noise grows higher, sharper—until it draws blood from his ears.

"SHUT THE FUCK UP!" he screams.

Everything stops. All the lights go out. The door slams shut.

He runs toward it, slamming his fists against the wood, but it won't move. Laughter fills the darkness.

"Who's there?" he cries.

A whisper answers, "Mine… you're mine… you have always been mine…"

The neighbor freezes, trembling. His eyes glaze over. Possessed, he turns toward the bathroom, walks to the tub, sits down, and slices his wrists. As blood spills, he chants softly, "Oh, my prayers are wasted… we are many…" Then, he collapses, dead—eyes staring blankly at the ceiling.

Moments later, the boy wakes. Disoriented, he stands, nearly seizing from the flashing lights. The dog spins in circles, excited that he's alive. As he looks around for his phone, he glances left—toward the bathroom—and sees the lifeless body sinking into the tub. The gurgling sound echoes until the body disappears completely. Then, a geyser of blood shoots upward, splattering across the ceiling.

The blood floods the room rapidly. The boy and the dog struggle to break down the door, the crimson tide rising to their knees. Desperate, the boy grabs something heavy to smash the window. His phone rings, but he ignores it, tucks it into his pocket, and shatters the glass.

He lifts the dog through first. She lands outside with a whimper. Without hesitation, he follows, cutting his feet on the shards. Bleeding and shaken, he limps toward the backyard gate, the dog beside him.

When they reach the front yard, a police officer pulls up—responding to a noise complaint. Seeing the boy and the dog covered in blood, the officer's expression turns from annoyance to alarm.

The boy and his loyal dog sit together on the curb—never to enter that house again.

Chapter 4: New People

Selling the house was easy, since all traces of the bloodshed were gone by the time the police investigated. Everything had returned to normal. So, a supposedly haunted house, now vacant and avoided by its former owner, eventually sold for cheap. Unlucky for the new buyers—a family of four: a father, mother, daughter, and their cat—who soon arrived at their new home.

The first to enter was the father, carrying a cage that held their anxious cat. The frightened animal took a while to come out, and being a male, immediately sprayed urine on the wall. With no other cleaning supplies on hand, the father wiped it up with an old sock from their luggage. He then took time to set up the TV they had brought in their car, since the moving company wouldn't arrive until the next day.

The house, still mostly empty except for its appliances, now echoed with the voices of four new inhabitants—each unaware of what awaited them.

None of them knew what would become of them, for the house took its time revealing itself, like a predator studying its prey. Many people fight for knowledge that ultimately destroys them, while others fight for nothing and die all the same. Knowledge can be both a blessing and a curse. As the Great Fire of Rome came and went, fear of being burned alive taught humanity how to protect itself—but the ultimate protection still rests with God.

The next day, when the movers arrived, they filled the house with everything that gave this family a sense of comfort and luxury—a privilege many billions would never know. Surrounded by their electronics and possessions, they settled into a false sense of security, unaware of how fragile it was.

For weeks, then months, nothing unusual happened. Life went on—until one afternoon, a cup fell from the kitchen counter, shattering on the floor and startling the mother.

She blamed it on carelessness—someone must have left it too close to the edge. Why assume anything else? As she cleaned up the shards, she accidentally cut her hand. A small drop of blood hit the floor. It was the first accidental bloodshed in the house since their arrival. She washed the cut, threw away the broken glass, and thought nothing more of it.

The next day, everyone left for work or school—forgetting one important thing: the front door was left unlocked.

Like a hunter setting its trap, the house waited patiently. Hours passed. People walked by, unaware. Then, a small sparrow landed on the sidewalk in front of the house, pecking at crumbs. The front door creaked open, and the curious bird hopped inside.

Once it was fully in, the door closed softly behind it. The sparrow froze when it saw two slit-like pupils staring from the shadows—the cat's eyes.

The cat pounced. The sparrow shot upward, wings flapping wildly. It darted through the house, chirping in terror, as the cat pursued it from room to room. Finally, the bird landed on top of a kitchen cabinet, thinking it had escaped. The cat leapt onto the countertop, knocking a stack of dishes to the floor.

Shattering glass echoed through the house. Both animals froze. The cat stared at the pile of broken plates for twenty long seconds before losing interest. The sparrow remained trapped above, chirping nervously for hours while the cat occasionally made half-hearted attempts to reach it.

Who would win—the cat or the little sparrow?

Then, a hollow groan reverberated through the house. The cat's fur bristled as it darted under the couch. Loud footsteps echoed from the front door, moving straight toward the living room.

The couch lifted into the air—held by an unseen force. The cat tried to run, but it was too late. It was yanked up by the tail, suspended in midair. A single, swift slice—from anus to neck— split the cat open. Its guts splattered to the floor before the lifeless body dropped beside them.

Hours later, the mother and daughter returned home. As they opened the front door, the sparrow shot past them, escaping into the sky.

The mother stepped inside first—and screamed. The daughter, right behind her, froze at the sight of her beloved pet mutilated on the carpet. Tears flooded her eyes as she fell to her knees.

The family immediately called the police, believing someone had broken in and killed the cat. The father arrived shortly after, and together they waited outside. The officers suggested they stay somewhere else for the night. Something about that house didn't feel right.

They checked into a nearby motel, making sure the house was locked tightly before leaving. Inside, only one thing stirred—the television, turning on by itself, repeating over and over:

"We... Are... Legion..."

The words echoed through the empty rooms until the day the family returned.

When they came back, they realized they had forgotten to clean the cat's bloodstain. The dark scarlet spot still marked the carpet. The parents noticed but ignored it. The daughter, however, grew uneasy.

Still mourning her pet, she went to bed early, hoping sleep would dull her sadness. The parents, tired from the move, decided not to clean that night either.

Then came the meowing.

Soft at first, coming from the living room. The parents, fast asleep, didn't hear it. The daughter did.

Quietly, she slipped out of bed, making sure to keep her blanket neat. She crept to the doorway and listened. The meowing was steady—almost rhythmic, like a heartbeat.

She tiptoed down the hallway, each step bringing her closer to the sound. The living room was dark. No sign of the cat. She looked around—nothing.

Suddenly, the television erupted in static, blaring loud enough to make her jump. Terrified, she ran back toward her room—but tripped, falling face-first and breaking her nose. She screamed in pain, but her cries were drowned out by the static and the eerie, rhythmic meowing.

Blood dripped down her face as she lay on the floor, trembling. Then her screams grew louder, waking her parents.

Everything went silent—except for the girl's sobs.

Her parents rushed into the hallway and found her crying, blood streaming down her face. The father knelt beside her, while the mother tried to calm her. When they told her to move her hands, they gasped at the sight of her mangled nose.

Panicking, the father ran back to the master bedroom, grabbed his car keys, and prepared to drive her to the hospital. The mother helped the girl to the living room couch, trying to understand what had happened.

Then the TV flickered on again, displaying words in static: **"We... Are... Legion..."**

The mother and daughter stared, confused and afraid.

A deafening roar suddenly erupted from the kitchen. Everything on the counters flew into the air and crashed to the floor. The father, hearing the chaos, tried to leave the bedroom—but before he could step out, the door slammed shut on his foot, crushing and breaking several toenails. He fell, writhing in pain.

The mother ran toward the door, shouting for him to open it, but it wouldn't budge.

The TV continued to hiss and distort, emitting sounds of animals—dogs, deer, rhinos—while heavy thuds shook the floor. Something massive was moving toward the girl.

The couch she sat on was suddenly flipped over, trapping her underneath. From above, pounding began—heavy, violent blows that made the wooden frame crack. The girl hyperventilated as whispers surrounded her:

"You don't have all the time in the world..."

The structure creaked and groaned, threatening to collapse on top of her.

In the bathroom, the father felt steam envelop him. The water had turned to blood, filling the room with a thick red mist. He coughed violently, unable to breathe or see. On the other side of the door, the mother screamed his name.

Then she heard a piercing whistle behind her.

She turned—and was grabbed by an invisible force that lifted her by the neck, choking her. She kicked and clawed, but it was no use. Her neck snapped with a sickening crack.

Inside the blood-soaked bathroom, the father stumbled to a bookshelf, grabbed a lighter, and ignited the flame. Fire roared to life, spreading rapidly through the room.

The entity screamed—a shriek so loud it shook the walls. Flames engulfed the house, consuming everything inside.

By the time authorities arrived, it was too late. The house was reduced to ashes.

They found only one survivor—the father, half-burned and broken, babbling incoherently about what had happened inside. No one believed him.

And the world remained blind—to the horrors lurking quietly in the neighborhood.

www.ingramcontent.com/pod-product-compliance
Lightning Source LLC
Chambersburg PA
CBHW040331020826
48978CB00013BC/1249